TEENAGE MUTANT NINJA TURTLES™

TRICKS AND TREATS

by Steve Murphy
illustrated by
Patrick Spaziante

Simon Spotlight
New York   London   Toronto   Sydney

E
Mur

Visit us at abdopublishing.com

Spotlight Library bound edition © 2007. Spotlight is a division of ABDO Publishing Company, Edina, Minnesota.

Simon Spotlight

An Imprint of Simon & Schuster Children's Publishing Division
1230 Avenue of the Americas, New York, New York 10020

ISBN-13 978-1-59961-250-8 (reinforced library bound edition)
ISBN-10 1-59961-250-X (reinforced library bound edition)

Library of Congress Cataloging-In-Publication Data
This book was previously cataloged with the following information:
  Murphy, Steve
    Tricks and Treats / by Steve Murphy ; illustrated by Patrick Spaziante.
      p. cm. -- (Teenage Mutant Ninja Turtles)
    ISBN 0-689-87058-2
    Summary: It's Halloween, and when the Turtles find out that the Purple Dragons have stolen candy from a bunch of kids, its time for some scary ninja tricks to get back all those treats.
    [1. Teenage Mutant Ninja Turtles (Fictitious characters)--Juvenile fiction. 2. Halloween--Juvenile fiction. 3. Halloween costumes--Juvenile fiction. 4. Heroes--Juvenile fiction.] I. Spaziante, Patrick, ill. II. Title. III. Series: Teenage Mutant Ninja Turtles ; #4.

[E]--dc22

2004303873

April opened her apartment door, letting in the Teenage Mutant Ninja Turtles.

"Boo-wah!" yelled Raphael, surprised at what he saw in the doorway.

"Jeepers-creepers!" Donatello exclaimed. "With an emphasis on *'creepers!'*"

"Happy Halloween!" greeted April. "Here you go, boys," she said, handing them each a decorated bag.

"Wow, great costumes, you two," said Leonardo, impressed.

"Yeah, but how come Casey's not wearing any monster makeup?" joked Raphael.

"Grrr. Not funny, little turtle," replied Casey Jones. He was trying to both look and *speak* like a monster.

"I can't believe you guys have never been trick-or-treating before," said April.

"Master Splinter never wanted us to leave the sewers when we were little," Leonardo replied.

"Right. But tonight we convinced him that looking like Ninja Turtles would be the perfect disguise on Halloween," added Donatello. "Everyone will think that we're wearing costumes."

The Turtles knocked on their first door of the night.

"You boys look so cute," said an old woman, as she opened the door and handed out chocolate bars.

"Cute? Really?" asked Raphael. His face fell.

"Well, no, not really," said the woman, noticing his disappointment. "You *really* look quite scary."

"Much better," replied Raphael, beaming.

The Turtles found a store that was giving out candy.

"Bring it on, dudes," said Michelangelo, stuffing both his bag and his mouth with candy.

"My stomach thinks this is the best holiday ever invented," said Michelangelo between mouthfuls of candy.

"Yug. Halloween good," agreed Casey, still trying to sound like a monster.

As they walked down the street, the Turtles met some children who were upset.
"What's wrong, little dudes?" asked Leonardo.
"Some bullies stole our candy," said a little girl dressed as a vampire.
"What! Where are they?" asked Raphael, outraged.
"They went thataway, I reckon," drawled the boy dressed up as a cowboy, pointing

Farther down the street a half-dozen Purple Dragons congratulated themselves.

"Just like stealing candy from a baby," said one Purple Dragon.

"It *was* stealing candy from a baby," laughed another Purple Dragon.

"I know of the perfect abandoned building right around the corner where we can chill out and look at our loot," said the Purple Dragon leader.

"They're heading into the old Poe building," said April. "It's supposed to be haunted."

"That gives me an idea," Leonardo said. "*We* could 'haunt' the Purple Dragons and scare them into giving up the stolen candy!"

Everyone agreed and set off to the Poe building.

The Turtles approached the house and went into ninja mode.

"Be like *shadows,* my brothers," whispered Leonardo with the softness of a breeze.

"Ahem," April said, clearing her throat.

"Right. My brothers and *sister,*" corrected Leonardo.

A short while later inside the abandoned building the Purple Dragons counted out their stolen candy.

"Wow! Look at all we got!" said one of them.

"And for *free*," said another. "Now who says that crime doesn't pay? Ha, ha, ha!"

"Hey! Where are you guys going?" asked the Purple Dragon leader.

"Exploring," answered a Purple Dragon, as he made his way out of the big central room. "Maybe there's other loot to be stolen from this fancy joint."

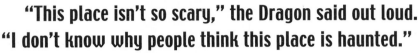

"This place isn't so scary," the Dragon said out loud. "I don't know why people think this place is haunted."

"I do," said a voice from the darkness in front of him.

Suddenly a face appeared!

"Because it *is* haunted!" said the face, scaring the Dragon who stood frozen with fear.

Meanwhile one of the Purple Dragons was poking around in the kitchen.
"There's the pantry," he said. "Maybe there's something to chow on besides candy."
He wasn't smart enough to remember that the house had long been *abandoned.*
"*Here's* something to chow on!" said Donatello in his best scary voice, leaping out from the pantry shadows.
The Purple Dragon fainted from fright.

Another one of the Dragons found a bathroom.

"What's *that*?" he asked, frightened by a dark shape behind the shower curtain.

"I . . . am . . . your . . . worst . . . *nightmare!*" growled April.

The Purple Dragon screamed.

The Dragon's scream tore through the house.

"Do you hear something strange?" asked the Purple Dragon leader.

"Never mind that," said one of the other Dragons. "What's that *other* sound? Like heavy footsteps . . . coming this way! I think this place really *is* haunted!"

Casey Jones lumbered toward the group of Dragons.

"UUUGGH! RARRRR!" moaned Casey in his deepest monster voice.

"Boo!" yelled Leonardo from behind a sheet, as he and Raphael leaped from the darkness.

"Boo-wah!" added Raphael.
The three Purple Dragons screamed in unison as they scrambled to get away.

"AAARRRGH!" all six of the Purple Dragons continued to scream, as they dropped their candy and ran out of the building.

"Bad guys gone," observed Casey.

"Yes, they are," agreed April. "We not only gave the Purple Dragons a good fright, but we also managed to get the kids' candy back."

"Everything except for what they ate," said Michelangelo, fighting the urge to eat the vast pile of candy before him.

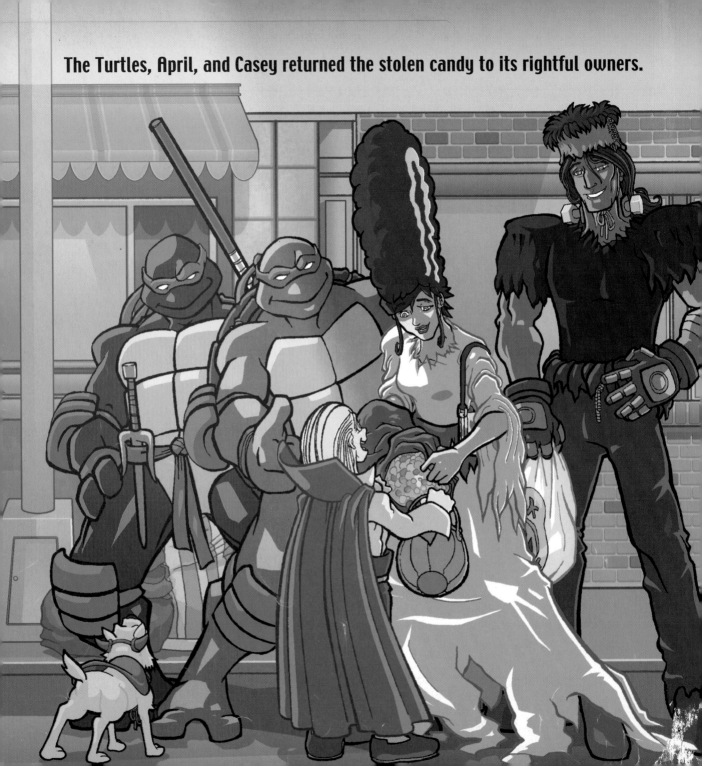

The Turtles, April, and Casey returned the stolen candy to its rightful owners.

"Wow! You got our candy back!" exclaimed the vampire girl.
"Thanks, partners," said the cowboy.

"We did a very good deed tonight," observed Donatello.

"We sure did," said Casey, tired of talking like a monster.

"Maybe that's why they say '*Happy* Halloween,'" joked Michelangelo.

Everyone smiled in agreement. It was a *very* happy Halloween!